AR
3.7

The AMAZING DAYS of ABBY HAYES®

Knowledge Is Power

Read more books about me!

The AMAZING DAYS of ABBY HAYES®

Knowledge Is Power

ANNE MAZER

AN
APPLE
PAPERBACK

SCHOLASTIC INC.
New York Toronto London Auckland Sydney
Mexico City New Delhi Hong Kong Buenos Aires

ISBN 0-439-63775-9

Text copyright © 2004 by Anne Mazer.
All rights reserved. Published by Scholastic Inc.

SCHOLASTIC, APPLE PAPERBACKS, THE AMAZING DAYS OF ABBY HAYES, and associated logos are trademarks and/or registered trademarks of Scholastic Inc.

12 11 10 9 8 7 6   5 6 7 8 9/0

Printed in the U.S.A.   40

First printing, July 2004

Thanks to all the girls who told me about sixth grade: Maddie, Kristina, Hannah, Cathie . . . and hi to Esther, Lydia, Maryiam, Julie, Hannah, and the many other Abby friends . . .

The AMAZING DAYS of ABBY HAYES®

Knowledge Is Power

Chapter 1

Wednesday

"Out with the old and in with the new."

That's what Mom said this morning when she announced Spring Cleaning in the Summer.

My siblings Alex, Isabel, Eva, and I will get rid of our outgrown clothes, toys, and books before we buy new clothes and supplies for school. We'll pack the old things in boxes and bring them down to the back porch. Dad and Mom will donate the stuff that's still usable to charity and throw out the rest.

<u>Out with the Old</u>
1. Frayed, ripped T-shirts
2. Purple jeans that are too small

3. Stuffed animals that I've had since kindergarten

4. Books that we've all outgrown
5. Papers from fifth grade
6. Card games with missing cards
7. Socks with holes

<u>In with the New</u>
1. A brand-new purple backpack!!!
2. Gel pens, fluorescent highlighters, mechanical pencils, scissors, erasers, glue sticks, notepads, a calculator, and other supplies
3. Pants: cute flared ones, with flowered designs. And maybe a skirt?
4. Tops: striped, lacy, gathered, and ruffled
5. New sixth-grade journals to write in
6. And . . . ?????

I earned lots of money this summer when I had to baby-sit Wynter, the difficult daughter of my mother's old college friend, Laurie.

Eva and Isabel said that sixth grade

was going to be easy after taking care of Wynter! They said I can handle anything now.

I hope they are right.

With the money I earned, I want to do something special for the "new" sixth-grade me. Here are some of my ideas:

1. Buy an electronic organizer. I can store all my friends' addresses and phone numbers in it and keep track of schedules and assignments.

2. Publish <u>The Hayes Book of World Records</u> for the world to read.

3. Print up my own calendar: <u>Abby Goes to Sixth Grade!</u> For my calendar, I'll take pictures of my friends, our new school, and our teachers, and I'll find inspiring quotes for every month. I have so many calendars now that I've lost track. Can I still use more? YES! Especially one that I've made myself.

4. Find a purple jacket and pants. (If I don't look like a giant eggplant.)

<u>New Things I WISH I Could Have</u>

1. My own laptop! (No explanation needed.)

    2. Pierced ears! (I have my own money to spend to have it done, but Mom <u>still</u> says no. I'm supposed to wait until the end of seventh grade, like Isabel and Eva.)

3. New hair! (I'm getting tired of my tangled, wild red curls. Why can't we change our hair as often as our outfits?)

I'd love to show up on the first day of school with pierced ears, straight dark brown hair, and a new laptop . . . no, I wouldn't bring it to school. But I'd tell everyone all about it!

"I can have *anything* in this box?" Hannah exclaimed. "For real?"

On her hands and knees, rummaging through another large cardboard box, Abby nodded. "I've already gone through it."

It was Thursday morning. Abby and her best

friend, Hannah, were sorting through Eva's and Isabel's throwaways on the back porch of the Hayes house.

They were ignoring Alex's boxes, which were filled with old sweatpants and one-armed robots. But Eva's and Isabel's boxes were treasure chests.

"Wow," Hannah said. "Look at all the nail polish Isabel threw out."

"Last year's colors," Abby explained.

Her older sister had a passion for polish. At any time, you could find hundreds of colors on Isabel's shelves. She polished her nails a new color daily.

"You don't want this, Abby?" Hannah held up a wool sweater.

"Isabel's clothes never fit me." Abby closed a box and opened another one. "She's so much taller than I am."

Hannah put the wool sweater on her pile.

"Eva threw out silver earrings." Abby held them up to her ears. "How do they look?"

"Earrings? Eva?" Hannah said.

Isabel's twin, Eva, was only interested in sports. All she had to give away were scuffed tennis shoes, muddy cleats, outgrown swimsuits, and dented water bottles.

"She probably got them as a present," Abby said. "And here's some bubble bath she never used."

"Flowered Splendor." Hannah took the bottle, unscrewed the cap, and took a sniff. "The Splendor is splendid. I think I might faint."

Abby giggled. She rummaged in the box again and pulled out a pair of enormous blue mittens. She tossed them into Hannah's lap.

"I could fit a small child into this mitten," Hannah said. "Who was Eva knitting for? A monster?"

"She made them when she was learning to knit," Abby explained. "She got the gauge wrong, and they came out three times too big."

"They'd be great for a snowman."

"One as big as a building."

Abby opened another box. She searched under some faded shirts and pulled out a small, battered notebook.

"It's an assignment book from Susan B. Anthony Middle School!" Abby cried. "Let's see how much homework they had every night."

"A lot, I bet!" Hannah groaned. "Middle school is so much harder than elementary."

"Sixth grade can't be *that* bad," Abby reasoned.

"Otherwise everyone would flunk out. They wouldn't do that to hundreds of kids, would they?"

"It depends on how evil the teachers are," Hannah said.

"They're not evil," Abby protested. "*You* should know!"

Both of Hannah's parents were teachers. Her mother taught kindergarten, and her father taught high school history.

"Neither of my parents has ever taught middle school," Hannah said.

Abby shrugged. "Eva and Isabel survived sixth grade."

"And what do they say about it?"

"Not much," Abby admitted. "But they keep telling me I'll do fine."

"They're covering something up," Hannah said. "Let me see that assignment book."

Abby handed her the book. Hannah opened it and gasped.

"Don't tell me!" Abby cried. "Six hours of homework a night? Long lists of vocabulary words to memorize? Pages of algebra?"

Hannah shook her head.

"*Worse* than that?"

"Does Isabel know what she threw out?" Hannah whispered.

"She probably got rid of a lot of stuff really fast."

"This is no assignment book."

"Is it her diary?" Abby cried. "Give it to me!"

Hannah returned the book.

Abby opened it to the first page.

Someone had drawn a picture of Susan B. Anthony Middle School, with a group of students standing outside.

The title read *Sixth Grade Revealed. The Inside Story! Written by Someone Who Knows THE TRUTH.*

Chapter 2

Thursday

"Knowledge is power."

Thinking Girl's Calendar

<u>Sixth Grade Revealed</u> is chock-full of knowledge.

Will this knowledge really give Hannah and me power?

What <u>kind</u> of power?

I am copying some of the book into my journal.

SIXTH GRADE REVEALED

Sixth grade <u>isn't</u> elementary school. It's not warm and fuzzy. No one holds your hand or wipes away your tears.

Last year you were the tallest and oldest in your school. This year, you're the shortest and youngest. Sixth grade is a whole new world. You have to master its rules to survive.

Popular People

Popular People are the pits. They are the worst. The meanest. They are the enemy of every average, normal sixth-grader.

The Popular People are a small minority, maybe one percent of the school population. But they have ALL of the power. They know how to rule and how to command. They bend other people to their will. Their friends, even the nice ones, often mysteriously turn out to be just like them: rotten.

popular person

Popular People are especially mean to anyone who's different. This means YOU.

If you're reading this, you are NOT a Popular Person. Here are some tips to avoid having this fact noticed:

<u>Don't</u>

—act superior to a Popular Person (even if you <u>are</u>!).

—disagree with a Popular Person (<u>all</u> the Popular People will gang up on you).

—try to make a Popular Person like you.

—pretend you're friends with a Popular Person.

—brag about how popular you are, <u>especially</u> if you're not.

—stand out from the crowd.

<u>Do</u>

—try to look older than your age.

—get a haircut in a new style.

—even better, change your hair color!

—listen patiently to endless conversations about boys, parties, and clothes.

—act like these things are very important.

—not ever stop smiling.

—use your wits. But not <u>too</u> much! The Popular People must never know how smart you really are.

Abby here again . . .

Use my wits — but not too much? How do you do THAT?

Now that I know some of the terrible things that can happen in sixth grade, I feel sick to my stomach.

The Popular People sound like Victoria and Brianna. They were the most popular girls in elementary school.

Brianna is always fashionably dressed. She's the star of every show. She takes private French lessons and goes for cruises on her family's brand-new boat.

Victoria is her best friend. She is also always fashionably dressed. She is not as good a dancer, singer, or actor as Brianna. But she is meaner.

Brianna and Victoria by themselves are bad enough. But a whole school ruled by them???

Help!!!

Chapter 3

Friday

"Ignorance is bliss."

Sleeping Dogs Calendar

YES, it is!

I wish I had never read <u>Sixth Grade Revealed</u>! I would have been MUCH happier without knowing what's waiting for me in middle school.

The book also has bad things to report about school lunches, getting lost, homework, bathroom passes, and gym class.

If only I could go on believing Eva and Isabel when they say that I'll do great! Now I don't believe a word of it.

Did Eva or Isabel write <u>Sixth Grade Revealed</u>?

Hannah and I don't think so.

They are both too ____.

Fill in blank with your choice of:

popular

perfect

brilliant

athletic

superior

sociable

dynamic

fearless

fabulous

flawless

to have written <u>Sixth Grade Revealed</u>.

<u>So how did Sixth Grade Revealed end up with Isabel?</u>

1. A friend left it in Isabel's room.

2. Isabel found it on the street.

3. It was a creative writing exercise.

4. It's actually a handbook for middle school on another planet, beamed into Isabel's room by a pointy-headed alien.

5. Explanation X. I can't imagine

how <u>Sixth Grade Revealed</u> ended up with my sister.

After reading <u>Sixth Grade Revealed</u>, I've concluded that there is only one thing for me to do. The old Abby will never survive in sixth grade.

I have to be a totally new person on my first day of middle school.

Clothes, hair, shoes, backpack, face—EVERYTHING!

old abby

"Let's go in that department store first," Eva said to Abby as they stood in the center court of the mall. "They have great sales."

"And we can find *everything* there," Isabel added.

"Are the clothes good?" Abby asked. "I *have* to change my look. And I'm counting on you to help me."

It was a week before school started. Abby's sisters had offered to take her shopping for middle school. She had eagerly accepted.

Since she had read *Sixth Grade Revealed*, school preparations had taken on a new urgency. She had gotten her hair cut shorter. She had started putting mousse in it every morning. She had secretly experimented with Isabel's tinted lip gloss. And she had painted her toenails.

No one would ever see them, but they made Abby feel more grown up.

"Don't worry," Isabel said. "This is a great store. And your personal fashion maven is here to guide you." She waved glittering turquoise nails in the air.

"I'll make sure all your choices are sensible, Abby," Eva said, with a meaningful glance at Isabel.

"Fashion is not incompatible with practicality," Isabel pronounced.

Eva rolled her eyes.

Abby wished her sisters wouldn't bicker. It was the main disadvantage of shopping with them.

She headed toward a rack of skirts. "Look!" she cried, holding out a pleated purple skirt. "What do you think?"

Isabel's frown disappeared. "I love it!" she cried.

"Isn't it a little teensy bit *bright*?" Eva said.

"Wear sunglasses," Isabel retorted.

Abby ignored them. She pulled out an open-necked shirt. "Is this a good match for the skirt?"

"Totally adorable," Isabel pronounced. "You'll look *so* cute for your first day."

"But she'd look cuter in jeans — and be more comfortable, too," Eva said.

"There is a place for beauty," Isabel pointed out. "And drama."

"I don't want to stand out *too* much!" Abby cried. Her head was starting to whirl from all the contradictory advice. "I just want to look like I belong."

Isabel grabbed her by the arm. "We're buying clogs, too," she said. "As soon as we're done with clothes shopping."

"For once, I agree," Eva said.

"You'll want to have comfortable shoes when you're running from class to class," Isabel explained.

"*Running?*" Abby said.

"You'll have plenty of time," Eva said.

"I'm getting nervous," Abby admitted.

She wondered if she should mention *Sixth Grade Revealed*. Or was it best not to say anything?

"You'll easily handle the worst of it," Isabel said.

"The worst?" Abby said in alarm.

Eva gave Isabel a dirty look. "There's *no* worst, Abby."

"You can handle anything," Isabel said. "After a week or two, you'll be so comfortable with middle school that you won't believe you were ever nervous about it." Isabel stopped at a rack of T-shirts. She pulled out a V-neck shirt with three-quarter-length sleeves. "Try on this, Abby!"

"Lime green?" Eva asked.

"At least it's not drab and dull," her twin shot back.

"I'm ready to try on the clothes," Abby said, hoping to distract her sisters from another argument.

Eva and Isabel continued to trade insults as they headed toward the changing room.

"Wait!" Abby cried suddenly. She hurried toward a glass counter. There was a large sign posted: FREE EAR PIERCING WITH PURCHASE OF ANY PAIR OF EAR-RINGS.

"Do you think . . . ?" she asked Isabel and Eva. Pierced ears were *exactly* what she needed for middle school. And besides, she had wanted them forever. "I have money from baby-sitting Wynter."

"You need the signed consent of an adult," Isabel said.

"Like an older sister?" Abby said hopefully.

Eva shook her head. "Like a parent. You know Mom wouldn't agree. And we're only fifteen years old."

"Oh, all right," Abby said. "I knew it wouldn't work."

Isabel thought for a moment. "Mom said you couldn't have pierced ears, but she didn't say anything about *not wearing* earrings, did she?"

Abby caught her breath. "What are you saying?"

"Why don't you buy a pair of clip-ons?" Isabel suggested. "It's not against Mom's rules, and no one in sixth grade will know the difference."

Abby looked from Eva to Isabel.

"*I* won't tell," Eva said.

"Me, neither," Isabel agreed.

"*Go for it,*" her sisters said in unison.

Chapter 4

Tuesday night

"What one has, one ought
to use . . ."

—Cicero

Storage Shed Calendar

TOMORROW IS THE FIRST DAY OF MIDDLE SCHOOL!

How I'm Using What I Have

1. I'm wearing the clogs, skirt, vest, shirt, and jewelry that I bought with Eva and Isabel.

2. My purple backpack with turquoise straps is loaded with new pens, notebooks, and a big, beautiful binder. I also put a new sixth-grade journal inside. Just in case I need to write!!!

3. I'm also using the secret pocket in my backpack. Inside are:

a) clip-on earrings
b) AND a new tinted lip gloss

I will put them on when I get to school.

Mom has never forbidden me to wear clip-on earrings or tinted lip gloss, so I'm not breaking any family rules. But I'm keeping them secret, anyway, in case Mom or Dad suddenly decides to make some NEW rules.

I feel more confident with my new clothes, new look, and new supplies.

Hannah has also made special preparations for the first day of school. She has a separate homework notebook and folders for each of her classes. Now that she has a system, she's not worried about homework.

We are going to walk to school with Casey and Mason.

About Casey

1. One of my best friends, even though he's a boy.
2. Funny. Likes to make jokes.
3. Loves sports.
4. Ignores when kids tease us and call us lovebirds. (It's NOT true!)

About Mason

1. A.K.a. "The Big Burper."
2. Tall, big. Dark curly hair.
3. Gross sense of humor.
4. Friends with Casey.

Casey's mother probably made him buy new clothes and get his hair cut. He hates new clothes! I wonder if he's worried about sixth grade, like me.

Knowing Casey, he'll be joking.

Will Mason still be the Big Burper in middle school? If he is, I'll pretend I don't know him.

Three Wishes for the First Day of Middle School

1. That all my teachers are wonderful
2. That I make a zillion new friends
3. That everything written in <u>Sixth Grade Revealed</u> is a lie

Today I am giving myself two extra quotes for good luck. (Like taking extra vitamins?)

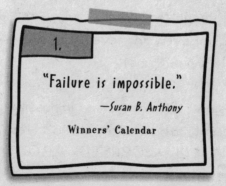

> **"Failure is impossible."**
> —Susan B. Anthony
> **Winners' Calendar**

<u>Prescription</u>: Repeat this quote one thousand times. Etch into brain. Write on palm of hand in purple ink. Take as often as necessary during first day of middle school.

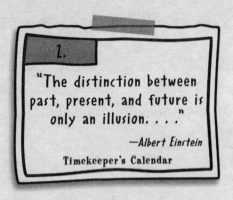

"The distinction between past, present, and future is only an illusion. . . ."

—Albert Einstein

Timekeeper's Calendar

A Thought: If past, present, and future are all the same, I've already started sixth grade. I've gotten through my first day. Maybe I'm even in seventh grade right now!!! (Ha-ha-ha-ha.)

Conclusion: If failure is impossible, and past, present, and future aren't real, WHAT AM I WORRIED ABOUT?
  Lots of things. . . .

Chapter 5

Wrong. Things change AND we change.

Elementary has changed to middle school (DUH!).

All the sixth-graders look really different. Like really, really, really, REALLY different. As if the middle school fairy waved a wand and made us all go POOF!

Girls: taller than boys. Suddenly slim or suddenly curvy. Much prettier, or much uglier.

Boys: have more muscles. Hair longer and more greasy (sometimes). Voices changing. Faces broader.

WHAT HAPPENED TO EVERYONE? Do I look different, too?

I hope I look cuter. And more fashion-able. And that everyone notices my clip-on earrings. I keep touching them to make sure they're still there. And my lips feel extrashiny with tinted lip gloss.

All the sixth-graders are in the auditorium now. No seventh- or eighth-graders are in school today, except a few who have vol-unteered to be guides. The sixth-graders will figure out the first day of middle school without the confusion of eight hundred other kids.

The principal is welcoming us to our new school. His name is Dr. Trane. He seems nice enough, but his speech is kind of bor-ing.

All the teachers are onstage with him.

Now they are introducing themselves. There are so many of them I can't keep track of their names. There are four gym teachers, five music teachers, one art teacher, a <u>lot</u> of social studies, science, and English teachers, too many math teachers, and NO creative writing teacher. (Boo-hoo!) But the librarian seems really enthusiastic and welcoming. I wonder if she knows Ms. Bunder, who taught creative writing in fifth grade. She was my favorite teacher, ever.

That's all I have time to write. The teachers are standing up to go back to their classrooms, and the bell is ringing. I have to go to my homeroom now.

In a crowd of sixth-graders, Abby pushed toward her English classroom. Her heart was pounding. She had lost track of Hannah a while ago. They had found themselves in the same social studies class earlier in the day, but no others.

Abby peered at the numbers on the door, then at the folded-up schedule she carried in her hand. A22, A24 . . . wasn't she supposed to be in B18?

"Excuse me," she said to a teacher standing at his door. "Where's B18?"

"Right down that hallway." He glanced at his watch. "You have just enough time to get there."

"Thanks!" Abby hurried in the direction he pointed.

"Faster! *Faster!*" said a familiar voice right behind her.

Abby whirled around. "Mason!"

"In person."

Even though that morning she had walked to school with him, she was still startled by his changed appearance.

Mason, too, had grown this summer. He was at least six inches taller than in fifth grade, but he hadn't gained any weight. Mason wasn't pudgy anymore. He was tall and slim.

"What class are you running to?" he asked.

"English in B18 with Ms. Schmidt."

"Me, too," Mason said. "Let's be late together."

"I want to be on time," Abby said, but she laughed, too.

It was good that Mason was in her class. In her last two classes, there hadn't been a single familiar face.

They rushed through the door of B18 just as the bell rang. Abby plunked herself down in the first seat she found.

Mason made his way to the back of the room.

"Two minutes to get yourself settled," Ms. Schmidt said. She was a small woman with long black hair in a ponytail. She looked energetic and friendly.

Abby unzipped her backpack, took out her new purple binder and pens, and placed them on her desk.

"So, Abby, you got your ears pierced," someone hissed.

Even a compliment from Victoria sounded like an insult. Abby wondered if middle school would improve her.

As usual, Victoria was dressed in the latest fashion. She wore slim flared pants and a spaghetti-strap tank top. Her arms and face were tanned. She had bangles on her wrists, and her lips were shiny and pink.

"Yes, I have earrings now," Abby said. It wasn't the whole truth, but it wasn't a lie, either. Her hand flew up to her clip-ons to make sure they were still there. If they fooled Victoria, they'd fool everyone.

"Where's Brianna?" Victoria demanded. "Have you, like, seen her?"

Abby shook her head. She had glimpsed Brianna once or twice in the hallway, always surrounded by admirers. But she hadn't been in any of Abby's classes.

"She's, like, supposed to be here, you know," Victoria said irritably. "She's so totally late. . . ."

As if on cue, the door opened, and Brianna made her entrance.

"Hello, everyone." Dressed in dazzling white to show off her tan and her dark hair, Brianna flashed her movie star smile. She didn't seem too worried about tardiness.

"You're just in time," Ms. Schmidt said. "Class is about to start."

"I'm *always* on time," Brianna announced. "It's my theatrical training." She flashed another brilliant smile at the class.

"Very nice," Ms. Schmidt said. She made a notation in her class notebook. "You'll be marked late if you arrive after the bell tomorrow."

Brianna tossed her hair dramatically and sat down next to Victoria.

"Like, where *were* you?"

Brianna smiled and didn't reply.

"I was, like, waiting!" Victoria's eyes narrowed to furious slits.

"So?" Brianna said. She examined her nails. They were perfect, of course.

"*No one* makes Victoria wait."

Brianna shrugged. "I had important things to do."

"Like *what*?" Victoria demanded.

"Maybe I have other friends besides *you*," Brianna said. "You're not the center of the universe, you know."

Victoria's face turned dark red. "Don't, like, expect me at your dumb-baby sleepover this weekend," she hissed.

"Fine," Brianna said.

"*Fine?*" Victoria repeated. She seemed stunned.

Before either of them could say another word, Ms. Schmidt clapped her hands for attention. She went to the chalkboard and began to write.

"These are the expectations I have for each student in my classes," Ms. Schmidt said. "You're expected to show up on time, pay attention, do the assignments, and hand them in on the due date. I have a format for assignments that must be followed strictly. Your name and class period go on the left. Underneath, you will write down the assignment topic and the date. The work must be *neatly* written by hand. No computers or typewriters."

The class groaned.

"That's right. No spell checks. You'll have to use the dictionary." Ms. Schmidt smiled. "I want you to copy these rules down in your notebooks and have your parents read and sign them tonight. At the bottom of the page. Right-hand side."

Abby glanced over at Mason. He pointed his finger at his forehead and twirled it.

Ms. Schmidt looked straight at Mason. "If you think that's crazy, it's your problem. This is my classroom, and you have to follow my rules. We're here to learn, and learning happens best in a disciplined environment. Welcome to middle school."

Welcome? Abby thought. She wanted to run to the nearest exit.

"When's lunch?" someone muttered.

Brianna took out a hot-pink electronic organizer and began to make notes on it.

"NO electronic devices allowed," Ms. Schmidt said. "Here we do things the old-fashioned way."

"Ha!" Victoria said.

Brianna shrugged and took out pen and paper.

"Too bad," Abby whispered in sympathy. She had wanted an electronic organizer, too, but at the last minute had spent her money on new clothes.

"Are you on *her* side, Abby?" Victoria demanded. "Or mine?"

"Neither."

"*Oh?*" Victoria said. Her voice was nasty.

"Stop it, Victoria," Brianna said in a bored voice. "Who cares, anyway?"

Victoria's eyes flashed in reply.

Abby sighed. Was she going to have to sit through a whole year of this? She glanced around the classroom and suddenly noticed a girl with long wavy hair that hid her face like a curtain. She was wearing a dark violet shirt and patched jeans and was doodling in a notebook.

Maybe Abby would sit near *her* next time. At least she was quiet.

"Okay, first homework assignment," Ms. Schmidt said. "Write it down."

The sixth-graders looked at one another in horror.

"Yes, homework," their teacher repeated. "Get used to it. To start the year, you're going to write personal narrative essays."

"Personal what-see?" someone said.

"A personal essay is an essay written by you, about you, in the first person."

A boy raised his hand. "Like, 'What I Did on My Summer Vacation'?"

Ms. Schmidt wrote a few more sentences on the board. "An essay should be thoughtful. In a personal essay, you try to make sense of your own experiences. I want you to write two pages about an event that changed your life, for better or worse. If that happened during your summer vacation, fine."

The sixth-graders hurried to write down their assignment. As Abby finished the last sentence, the bell rang again. She threw her assignment notebook into her backpack.

Everyone rushed to their next class. Abby followed the crowd. In sixth grade, no one even had time to catch their breath.

Chapter 6

A crowd ISN'T company! I'm alone in the midst of hundreds of people. Of all the kids in the cafeteria right now, there's not a single familiar face.

A few minutes ago, I stood in the cafeteria line and bought lunch for the first time. It's spaghetti and sauce and cheese, with mushy green beans and a tiny slice of chocolate cake. The milk, at least, tastes normal.

<u>Sixth Grade Revealed</u> was right about the school lunches! They're bad. But so far, sixth grade has been mostly okay.

I haven't gotten lost. I haven't been late to a single class. I opened my locker easily. I memorized the combination easily, too. I have all the right supplies. I feel good in my new clothes and earrings.

So far, my teachers seem nice. I might even like Ms. Schmidt.

The teachers all have different requirements. Some want all papers typed; others want them neatly handwritten. Some give homework every night; others twice a week. Some hand out schedules in advance; others assign day-to-day. They keep telling us that by the end of the week, we'll have it all figured out. It might take me more than a week. But I'm not as overwhelmed as I thought I'd be.

Could Sixth Grade Revealed be mostly lies? Even the stuff about the Popular People? Maybe it's just out of date.

My first scary moment was five minutes ago.

When I exited the lunch line, I looked around at the tables full of strangers. Then I sat down quickly at an empty table.

I kept thinking that if Hannah were here, she would have joined a group of strangers and made ten new friends already. And I would have made friends with them, too. But Hannah has a different lunchtime!

My table is next to the window. I can stare at the concrete courtyard outside and pretend that I see something fascinating. I hope someone joins me soon.

A girl is putting her tray on my table. She is sitting down across from me. It's the girl in the violet shirt from Ms. Schmidt's class. Hooray!

Abby closed her journal and slipped it into her backpack. She looked at the girl, then down at her tray again.

"Um," Abby began. She pretended to clear her throat.

The girl didn't say anything. She concentrated hard on her lunch, taking slow bites of the spaghetti on her tray.

"Um, hi," Abby repeated a little more loudly.

The girl didn't respond. To her left was a battered

and worn notebook, with elaborate doodles on the cover.

Abby wondered if it was a journal like hers or just a school notebook.

Maybe the girl hadn't heard her. Abby gathered her courage to speak up again. But just as she opened her mouth, the girl jumped up, threw the remains of her lunch in the trash, and hurried out of the cafeteria.

Abby stared after her. Had the girl even noticed her?

"Abby! You got pierced ears!"

"They're actually clip-ons," Abby confided. "Don't tell."

Abby's friend Bethany caught up with her in the hallway between classes.

Abby was happy to see her. Even though it was only hours, it felt like *weeks* since she had seen a friendly face.

Especially after that girl ran out of the cafeteria. Abby knew it probably wasn't personal, but she felt discouraged, anyway.

"The clip-ons fooled *me*," Bethany said. She had gotten taller over the past few months, and her blond

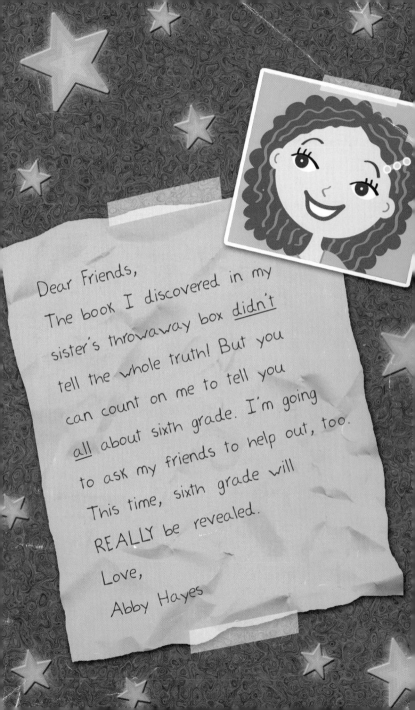

Dear Friends,

The book I discovered in my sister's throwaway box <u>didn't</u> tell the whole truth! But you can count on me to tell you <u>all</u> about sixth grade. I'm going to ask my friends to help out, too. This time, sixth grade will REALLY be revealed.

Love,
Abby Hayes

Natalie's Tips on Getting Organized:

1. Have a special homework notebook divided into sections for each class.
2. Write down your homework assignments very carefully every day.
3. Review your notebook when you get home.
4. Check off completed homework assignments on a calendar.
5. Put your homework assignments in a special folder so you don't lose them.
6. Find a quiet place at home or school to do your homework.
7. If you get behind, talk to your teacher and work out a makeup schedule.
8. In school, don't just throw everything to the bottom of your locker. If you hang things up, they'll be easier to find.
9. Remember to bring gym clothes on gym days. Or store them in your locker.
10. When you run out of supplies, don't wait until the last minute to get new ones!

I can't believe that Natalie wrote all these tips! Where did she learn this stuff???

I tried a few of her ideas, like checking off completed homework assignments on a calenda It works! No more forgotten homework assignment But I still throw everything on the bottom of my locker.

Hannah's Friendship Tips:

1. Smile and say hello.
2. When you meet new people, ask questions about what they like.
3. If someone is shy, take time to listen.
4. Offer to help if someone is lost or confused.
5. If your best friend isn't in any of your classes, walk home from school together. Or sit together on the bus or set a special time to talk.
6. You can leave notes or cards in your friends' lockers during the day.
7. Ignore bullies. If they won't leave you alone, speak to a trusted teacher, parent, or guidance counselor.
8. If you're in a new school and don't know anyone, join a fun activity.
9. Look for friends who have similar interests to you, like music, sports, or arts.
10. Be a good friend. Don't tell other people's secrets or talk behind their backs.

I think Hannah's already made friends with the entire sixth grade! (How does she _do_ that?) The last time I met someone new, I took Hannah's advice and asked lots of questions. I discovered that she loves purple too, and also has an obnoxious older sibling who's sports star. Yesterday she introduced me to two of h friends. Now I have three new friends!! Hooray!!!

Brianna's Fashion Tips:

ay tuned for the publishing event of the year! It's called
Brianna's Book of F.A.M.E. (Fashion, Accessories, Makeup,
and Elegance); or <u>365 Days of Outstanding Outfits.</u>
My cousin's uncle's nephew's aunt's husband's
grandmother's best friend's niece photographed me in
365 fabulous outfits, with full makeup, accessories, and the
latest hairstyles. It's the best and it's coming soon to
a bookstore near you! Make sure you get your personally
autographed copy! It will be THE book you read over and
over and over again. . . .

Sigh. Like, why did
ask <u>them</u>? Here
e a few fashion
s I collected from
s in the cafeteria
lunch yesterday: A Sampler of Super Sixth
ade Fashion Tips:

VICTORIA'S FASHION TIPS:
Like, why should I tell <u>you</u>?

ipes forever!

Make sure your
eye makeup matches
your toenail polish.

Wear dark
clothes for
cafeteria food
fights.

Untie your
sneakers.

Strappy sandals
aren't a good idea
in gym class.

ha-ha. Who wrote these, anyway? No wonder they aren't signed!

Bethany's Tips for Gettin' Along with Teachers:

1. Write down what each teacher expects from their students.
2. Follow their instructions carefully.
3. Ask questions if you don't understand an assignment.
4. Turn in work on time.
5. Listen and take notes in class.
6. Participate and raise your hand.
7. Do your share of work on group projects.
8. Don't chew bubble gum in class.
9. Don't stare at the clock, either. Or yawn. Or sleep at your desk. Or do your nails. Or pass notes. Or yell. Or play handheld games.
10. Remember: The teacher wants you to succeed. Ask for help if you need it.

Are there actually kids who sleep at their desks, yell, or do their nails during class? Wow (I sometimes pass notes, but only when I absolutely <u>have</u> to!)

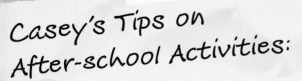

Casey's Tips on After-school Activities:

1. Research all the choices: sports, arts, theater, music, special interest clubs, and lots more.
2. Choose one or two activities that you really enjoy or that you want to try.
3. Write the dates down for your parents and let them know when you'll be home late, or when you need rides.
4. Don't over-schedule yourself! Leave time for homework and relaxing.
5. You'll meet lots of new friends and gain new skills.

Lots of my friends are involved in after-school clubs or activities. Casey plays soccer, basketball, and baseball, and writes a cartoon for the school newspaper. Natalie is involved in the school musical. Brianna is president of the French Society. Bethany started a group called Future Veterinarians. Hannah is checking out the Young Scientists. Mason joined a magic club. Is there a club for purple-journal writers?

Mason's Tips on How to Deal with Bullies

1. Don't take it personally.
2. Don't try to make the bully like you or argue with them.
3. Ignore the bully or walk away.
4. Ask for help from parents, teachers, or counselors.
5. No, this never happened to me, but I watched a lot of my friends go through it. It's really hard on them.

Inside the Big Burper is a wise friend.

More of Mason's Terrific Tips:

1. Speak loudly and carry a big backpack.
2. To clear crowded hallways, announce that you've just been exposed to a highly contagious disease.
3. Don't burp in the middle of the principal's speech.

Forget what I just wrote! The Big Burper will never change.

THE FUNNIEST THINGS ABOUT SIXTH GRA

science teacher.
—Natalie

Paper airplane fights in the cafeteria.
—Mason

Boys' squeaky voices in chorus.
—Brianna

Everyone in the hallways between classes, like the subway at rush hour.
—Hannah

Watching kids try to act cool.
—Victoria

Backpacks that are bigger than the kids who carry them.
—Abby

Eating lunch at 10:15 in the morning.
—Bethany

Mason's jokes.
—Casey

THE SCARIEST THINGS ABOUT SIXTH GRA

The inside of my backpack.
—Mason

Mason at the lunch table.
—Casey

Forgetting my makeup.
—Brianna

Our reading list for English class.
—Bethany

Like, why do you want to know?
—Victoria

When I can't find where I put my homework assignments.
—Hannah

All the new rules.
—Natalie

Mean kids.
—Abby

HE MOST SURPRISING THINGS ABOUT SIXTH GRAD

w tall the girls are.
—Casey

How short the boys are.
—Hannah

Like, what's so sur-prising? Sixth grade is so totally boring.
—Victoria

There are actually people who haven't heard of me.
—Brianna

My teachers are great.
—Natalie

I haven't gotten a single detention.
—Mason

I made five new friends.
—Bethany

Everyone changed so much!
—Abby

hair had streaks from the sun. She looked tanned and healthy and strong.

"Don't tell anyone!"

"I won't," Bethany promised. "Are you sorry the summer is over? I spent my time mucking out stalls and feeding cows. I *loved* it!"

Abby sighed. "I had to watch a really awful kid. But I earned a lot of money from it. The rest of the time I relaxed."

"Cool," Bethany said.

"We're all here!" Natalie cried joyfully. Bethany's best friend hurried to catch up with them.

Abby stared at Natalie. "You've *changed*," she said.

In fifth grade, Natalie had had short dark hair. She wore rumpled clothes that were frequently stained and socks that didn't match.

Now, in sixth grade, her hair was cut in a sleek bob. She wore a black scoop-necked shirt and slim-cut black pants. She wasn't wearing her trademark paint-splattered sneakers but sported new leather boots.

The messiest girl in fifth grade now looked as if she had stepped out of a magazine advertisement for middle school.

"You look like a different person," Abby said again. She couldn't take her eyes off Natalie. "Are you still you?"

Natalie shrugged. "Here's my classroom. Are either of you in chorus this period?"

Bethany's eyes lit up. "Me!"

"Not me. I have health class," Abby said. "It's somewhere around here."

"I wish you were with *us*," Bethany said.

"Me, too!" Abby said.

Natalie pointed to her watch. "Better hurry! The bell's about to ring!"

Abby waved good-bye and walked quickly down the hallway.

Ahead of her, the girl with the violet blouse appeared in a crowd of kids and then disappeared.

The bell rang with a loud, obnoxious bleat. Abby began to run. Her backpack bounced up and down as she searched for the right classroom. Finally, she spotted the door.

With a final burst of speed, Abby dashed into the classroom. Her feet slipped on the polished floor. Abby tottered, lost her balance, and flew into the air. She landed squarely on her back.

Thirty students stared in astonishment.

Chapter 7

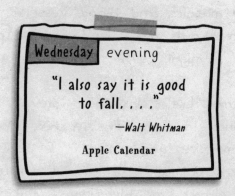

Wednesday evening

"I also say it is good
to fall. . . ."

—Walt Whitman

Apple Calendar

Good?

Did he ever fall on
the first day of middle
school with an entire
roomful of strangers goggling at him?

Did he land flat on his back with the
breath knocked out of his body and everything hurting?

Did he make the most dramatic and hu-
miliating entrance EVER in the history of
health class?

(What IS health class, anyway? Do we

study food groups and proper diet? Or memorize muscles and blood vessels? Or do we learn about safety and how to prevent injuries? I might be the first lesson!)

It seemed like I lay there forever. I was too stunned to move. The teacher, Ms. Newman, came over and asked if I was okay.

I slowly got up. My legs were bruised, and my elbow was bleeding. I felt shaky and ready to cry.

Worst of all, I was completely embarrassed. What had happened to me was so awful that even Sixth Grade Revealed hadn't thought of it.

"Go to the nurse's office and get your arm cleaned up," Ms. Newman said.

I couldn't speak.

"The nurse will give you an ice pack for your bruise." She wrote a few words on a pass. "Leave your backpack here. Take it easy. Go slow. Don't fall again."

Someone snickered.

"Will another student accompany her to the nurse's office?" Ms. Newman asked.

"Volunteers, please."

A girl came to the front of the room. My eyes were too blurry with tears to see who it was.

"Make sure she's okay," Ms. Newman said to my student bodyguard. "Help her on the stairs."

"Like, sure."

I wiped my eyes and looked up.

Victoria stood in front of me.

She took me by the arm and led me into the hallway. As soon as we were out of sight, she let go of me.

"Like, I'm so totally glad you fell, Abby!" she sneered. "I get to, like, skip out of another boring class. That teacher didn't even figure out that we, like, know each other, you know."

Victoria started laughing.

"What's so funny?"

"You looked so totally ridiculous lying on the floor. All the boys were, like, making fun of you."

"My leg really hurts. And so does my arm."

Victoria smiled meanly. "Don't worry. You'll get a Band-Aid on your ouchie in the nurse's office."

"I don't have ouchies, I have boo-boos," I retorted.

"Huh?" She suddenly brightened. "Abby! Like, I think you've lost something."

"My dignity?" I muttered.

"Your earring," Victoria announced triumphantly. "You're a one-earring wonder."

My hands flew to my ears. One clip-on earring was still there; the other was gone.

"<u>Pierced</u> ears?" Victoria sneered. "I knew it wasn't true. Wait until I tell everyone."

I Know It's Hard to Believe, but Things DID Get Worse

The nurse wasn't exactly sympathetic. She scolded me for running in the halls. Apparently some kid once broke a leg in school. She said it was my own fault if I did, too, and that it wouldn't be any fun having my leg in a cast for three months at the beginning of the school year.

(She actually made me feel grateful that I had only bruised myself.)

Then she put a stinging disinfectant on my elbow, and it stained my new shirt.

I couldn't have an aspirin without a medical release form from my parents. She taped an ice pack on my leg and told me to take a pain reliever when I got home.

Victoria laughed at my clip-on earrings all the way back to class.

When we got there, I had to listen to her call me the one-earring wonder. Some kids thought it was pretty funny.

She also made up a song about me.

"She flies through the air with, like, the greatest of ease,

"The one-earring girl who falls down on her knees."

It's, like, a TOTALLY stupid song, and, you know, I think Victoria should, like, take the word <u>like</u> out. And it isn't even accurate. I <u>didn't</u> fall on my knees, I fell flat on my back. Not that _that_ matters to Victoria and her friends.

On top of everything else, I never found my missing earring.

Chapter 8

Wednesday still

"Everything's got a moral, if only you can find it."

—Lewis Carroll

Looking Glass Calendar

Oh, really?

Even falling down in health class and looking like a complete idiot, then losing a clip-on earring and being exposed as an ear-piercing fake? And being teased by Victoria and her friends for the rest of the day?

Okay, I'll try to find a moral in this. I have nothing better to do. Except my homework.

<u>Moral</u>

1. Walk, DON'T run into health class, even if you're late.

2. Make sure clip-on earrings are fastened with superglue or cement. Even if you fall, they won't.

3. Never accept help from Victoria, especially after she's had a fight with Brianna. (She seemed about ten times as mean as usual.)

4. Have dark sunglasses and disguise ready in case something like this happens to you.

5. Consult <u>Sixth Grade Revealed</u> for hints on how to deal with this.

6. On the other hand, DON'T consult <u>Sixth Grade Revealed</u>. It's too depressing.

7. Never pretend that your ears are pierced when they aren't.

Hmmm. Maybe I can write my personal narrative essay about this event. It has changed my life, and I have learned something from it.

<u>Another Moral or Two</u>
1. Get your ears pierced <u>for real</u>!
2. SOON!

Help! Is middle school all over for me before it's really begun?

"I *don't* want to go to school today!" Abby said to Hannah. It was Thursday morning. The two girls stood on a street corner waiting for Mason and Casey to join them.

Hannah looked sympathetic. "I wouldn't, either, if I were you," she admitted.

Abby touched the tip of her bare earlobe. She had left all earrings at home today.

"Everyone is going to know me as the one-earring wonder!" Abby cried. "*Why* didn't my mother let me get my ears pierced this summer?"

"For the same reason mine didn't." Hannah flung her arm around Abby's shoulder. "Don't worry — it'll be okay!"

Abby frowned. "Last night I begged my mom to change her mind."

"And?" Hannah said.

"She didn't even *hear* me," Abby said, sighing deeply. "Her head is filled with details of a clothing drive she's organizing."

"Did she say *anything*?"

"Only that there are kids in this city who don't

49

have warm coats or gloves for winter. I felt stupid for even asking about pierced ears."

"But doesn't she understand?" Hannah cried. "What did she say when you told her about Victoria?"

Abby turned red. "I didn't tell her."

"Why not?"

"Too embarrassed," Abby mumbled. "This never happens to my perfect sisters."

"Are you sure?"

"*Sure,*" Abby said. There was *no way* that she would admit to her family that Victoria was picking on her.

"I bet your mother would help you if she knew . . ." Hannah began, then stopped. "Here come Mason and Casey."

The two boys were approaching the intersection. Mason was telling a story to Casey, who was doubled over with laughter.

"Don't tell them about Victoria," Abby whispered.

"Why not? They're our friends."

"No," Abby repeated. "*Don't.*"

As a joke, Mason pretended to stumble across the street. He landed on his knees in front of the girls.

"I beg you!" he cried. "Lollipops! I'm dying for lollipops. Have pity on a poor sixth-grader!"

"Get up," Hannah said, laughing. "We don't have any."

"No lollipops here," Abby agreed.

"Hey, Hayes," Casey said.

"Ho, Hoffman." In spite of herself, Abby sighed.

Casey glanced at her. "Anything wrong?"

"Nothing," Abby said quickly. "Just school starting. Summer ending. That sort of thing."

"URP!" Mason burped.

"Gee," Hannah complained, "don't you ever take a vacation?"

Mason rose from his knees. "Today at lunch, I'm letting loose the Big One," he announced. "It's going to set off seismic waves in the cafeteria."

"Wowee," Hannah said.

Mason grinned. "I'm exhibiting my class A for Astonishing talent at Victoria's table. I hope all her friends are, like, so totally horrified, you know."

Abby stared at Mason. "You are? *Why?*"

"To express my deep and abiding feelings for Victoria," Mason said.

"That we all share," Casey added.

Mason looked at Abby and said in a low voice, "I heard what happened yesterday."

"Me, too," Casey said. "It stinks."

Abby covered her face with her hands and groaned.

"We want to do something," Mason said.

"No," Abby said. The last thing she needed was Mason burping in her defense. "*Please* don't. It'll only make things worse."

"I've got it!" Hannah's eyes sparkled. "What if we all wear one earring to school tomorrow? Let's make it a badge of pride! Or an earring of pride," she corrected.

"NO!" Mason said firmly.

"I'm *not* wearing earrings," Casey said. "For anything or anyone. Even Abby."

"Let's not do *anything*," Abby said. "I mean, it's great that you want to stick up for me, but I don't want to be the center of attention."

"You already are," Casey pointed out.

"He's right," Hannah agreed. "Let the world know that you won't take this lying down."

"I already *was* lying down," Abby said. "When I slipped in health class, remember?"

"Maybe we can *all* fall down," Casey proposed.

"I like that," Mason said. "Stuntmen for a cause."

"Not a bad idea," Hannah said.

"Can we just forget about this?" Abby begged her friends. "Today is a new day. Maybe things will be different."

But somehow she didn't think so.

"Don't you want to *do* something?" Hannah said.

"Yeah, I want to get my ears pierced," Abby said. "That would stop a lot of the teasing."

"Why don't you?" Mason asked.

Abby frowned. "I'm supposed to wait until the end of seventh grade. A family rule."

"Too bad," Casey said.

"I'm ready to break the rule," Abby said desperately. "If I could find someone to do it without signed permission from my parents."

"My older sister pierces ears at the mall," Mason said. "I bet she'd do it for you."

Chapter 9

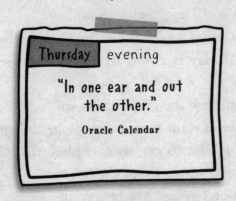

Thursday | evening

"In one ear and out the other."

Oracle Calendar

On the way to school, Hannah and Casey tried to talk me out of piercing my ears without my parents' permission.

<u>Hannah</u>

1. Talk to your family first, explain the situation, and see if they'll change the rules. (Right. Yeah.)

2. Having your ears pierced will not change Victoria. (But it'll change <u>me</u>.)

3. It'll get you in trouble. (<u>So?</u>)

4. Maybe it'll make things worse. (Impossible.)

5. Trust your friends. They'll help and support you. (Okay, but this is my problem, and I have to solve it.)

<u>Casey</u>

1. Pretty much the same advice as Hannah. (Okay, okay.)

2. Why not beat Victoria at her own game? Make up an even funnier song and sing it. (NO WAY!)

Their arguments went in one ear and out the other.

Only Mason didn't try to change my mind. He said that, considering the circumstances, he didn't blame me for what I was going to do.

"Desperate times demand desperate actions," Mason said, burping to punctuate his statement.

I told Mason I'd use his quote on my <u>Abby Goes to Sixth Grade</u> calendar, if I ever made one. If I ever <u>survived</u> sixth grade.

Then we arrived at school. Everything had changed again.

*   *   *

Yesterday the sixth-graders looked as if they had been sprinkled with fairy dust. Today we've all <u>shrunk</u>. Have we gone through the looking glass? Are we in a fairy tale? (I WISH! Then Victoria would have snakes and toads coming out of her mouth every time she sang her mean song.)

The seventh- and eighth-graders are here, and they're HUGE! Could they be college students in disguise?

Hannah grabbed my arm. "Now that the seventh- and eighth-graders are back, Victoria will forget all about you."

"Do you really think so?" I said.

Casey agreed. "She doesn't have a good attention span."

"But who would have thought that Victoria could compose a rhyme, set it to music, teach dozens of kids, and sing it for the rest of the day?" I argued.

Mason laughed. "You've brought out her hidden talents!"

"Boy, that makes me feel better," I said sarcastically.

"Don't worry," Hannah said. "This will work out. Somehow."

The four of us walked toward the front door. A group of kids were huddled together in a tight knot. Suddenly, they sprang apart. Victoria emerged from their center. She saw me, grinned nastily, and motioned to the group. They hummed together and began to sing, "One earring, two ears . . ."

The seventh- and eighth-graders stared. So did Brianna, who was surrounded by a group of girls who looked like supermodels. They pointed at Victoria and whispered.

Victoria looked at Brianna and the other girls. An expression of pure rage crossed her face. Then she walked toward my friends.

"Abby lied about having pierced ears," she said loudly so Brianna could hear. "Is that, like, the most totally PATHETIC thing you've ever heard?"

"Shut up, Victoria," Mason said.

Victoria laughed and walked away.

I turned to Mason. "That's it," I said. "Call your sister. As soon as you can. I want my ears pierced."

Mason and Abby and Hannah walked through the mall, glancing at windows that displayed shoes, perfumes, and winter coats.

The three friends had taken a bus to the mall after school on Friday. They had told their parents they were going to a bookstore and had promised to be home by dinnertime. Only Casey hadn't been able to join them because of a doctor's appointment.

"The store is over here," Mason said, pointing to the left. "If it hasn't moved again."

This is it, Abby thought. This is the moment I've been waiting for. Finally — pierced ears! She had wanted pierced ears for as long as she could remember. But she had never thought that it would happen like this.

Hannah adjusted the strap of her backpack. "This is kind of exciting," she said. "Even though it's dangerous and probably wrong."

"Do you have enough money to buy a pair of earrings?" Mason asked Abby. "That's the deal. Free ear piercing with the purchase of any earrings."

"I sure do," Abby said, patting her pocket. "Does your sister know what she's doing?" she asked nervously.

"She's done it millions of times. And they have a machine that does it in a minute. You choose the studs and then, bam, pierced ears. It's very safe with modern technology and know-how."

"Wow," Hannah said. "My mom had it done at a doctor's office. They didn't have a machine. They had to use a sterilized needle and ice. She took the earrings out too soon and the holes closed up."

"I'm not taking them out," Abby promised. "*Ever.*"

"Unless your parents make you," Hannah said.

Abby scowled. "They better not!"

"You'll have to use an antiseptic solution to clean them every day," Mason warned.

"Of *course*," Abby said.

"Mason, you're a pierced ear expert," Hannah teased.

He grinned. "I love the gory details."

They stopped in front of a store window lettered

with sparkling pink and purple. Inside there were racks of earrings, vinyl purses, lipsticks, hair ornaments, and makeup packaged in glittering cases. A tall girl with dark hair was behind the counter, ringing up a purchase. Other than that, the store was nearly empty.

The customer walked out with her package. The tall girl ducked down behind the counter.

"We're here," Mason said.

"Is that Kathleen?" Abby asked.

"My big sis," Mason said proudly. "Shall we go in and do the deed?"

"You can still change your mind, Abby," Hannah cautioned. "It's not too late. Don't do it if you'll be sorry later."

Abby looked at her friends. She thought of what her parents would say. She thought of what her sisters would say. Then she thought of how Victoria kept taunting her and calling her a one-earring wonder. She remembered all the seventh- and eighth-graders who had heard it.

Pierced ears were her first line of defense. She would feel so much more confident with them.

Abby took a deep breath. "Yes," she said, "I want to do it."

Chapter 10

I did it.

I did it.

I did it.

I did it.

I DID IT!

I DID IT!

I now have pierced ears. And totally adorable tiny gold earrings that I have to clean with antiseptic solution twice a day.

When Kathleen saw the three of us walk into the store, she glanced around nervously.

No one else was in the store. Then she said, "Let's do this quickly. I could lose my job."

Kathleen looked into my eyes. "I'm taking a **big** risk here. In fact, I'm crazy to do this in the first place."

"I won't say a word!" I promised. "You can count on me!"

Kathleen nodded. "Do you have your gold posts picked out?"

I handed them to her. She put them into the ear-piercing gun one at a time.

"A gun?" I said. "That seems violent."

"It's not violent at all. It happens in the blink of an eye. You won't believe how quick and easy it is," Kathleen promised. "Don't worry. I've done it hundreds of times."

She cleaned my earlobes, picked up the gun, and . . .

OUCH!!! OUCH!!!

My earlobes turned bright red (said Hannah). They stung like a bee had pierced them. The machine sounded like a stapler.

When I looked in the mirror, I had pierced ears.

"They look really great," Hannah said admiringly. "Maybe I should get mine pierced, too."

"No way! Not without your parents' permission!" Kathleen cried. "I'm only sticking my neck out once."

"Thanks for doing it," I said. "I really, really, really, really, really appreciate it!"

Kathleen peeled off her surgical gloves. "I hope that Victoria gets a taste of her own medicine," she said.

Then she made me solemnly promise three things:

1. To follow all the instructions on the sheet she gave me about taking care of my pierced ears.

2. To NEVER reveal who pierced my ears, no matter what.

3. If my ears get infected, to remove the earrings and see either a doctor or the school nurse right away.

I thanked Kathleen about a billion times more and then paid her for the gold ear-rings, antiseptic solution, and a couple of wide, stretchy headbands and cute hats (to hide pierced ears from family, of course).

By the time we left the store, my ears didn't sting anymore.
We still had an hour and a half to spend at the mall before it was time to catch the return bus.

<u>Hannah, Mason, and Abby's Afternoon at the Mall</u>
1. The Bookstore
Hannah and I found a series to read. It's called <u>The Terrific Times of Julie Hymes</u>. It's all about the adventures of a group of middle school friends. It's real-istic and funny – my favorite kind of

story! I bought the first three books of the series.

Then we listened to CDs in the record section.

2. The Pretzel Store

I treated everyone to giant hot pretzels and sodas and had a moment of gratitude for my friends.

If it hadn't been for Mason, I wouldn't have gotten my ears pierced at all.

And Hannah came with me even though she didn't agree with my decision.

My friends are the **BEST**!

3. The Mall Stroll

We wandered through the mall eating our pretzels and looking for mirrors so that I could admire my new earrings.

4. The Bus Stop

We arrived at the bus stop just as the bus pulled up. We hopped on, found three seats together, and sat down. All of us opened our new books and read until it was time to get off at our stop.

When we got off the bus, I tied a scarf around my head to hide my pierced ears. Then we walked home.

Chapter 11

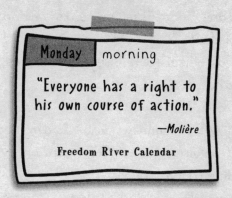

Monday morning

"Everyone has a right to his own course of action."

—Molière

Freedom River Calendar

Or hers!

Abby's Action Plan

When parents discover pierced ears, I will do the following:

1. Show them this quote.
2. Announce that I did it all on my own initiative.
3. Explain that times have changed since Isabel and Eva were in sixth grade and it is now NECESSARY for any self-respecting sixth-grade girl to have pierced ears.

4. Tell them that "What's done cannot be undone," or "Pierced ears cannot be unpierced."
5. If all else fails, beg. On knees, if necessary.
6. Or cry.
7. Do NOT explain why I am begging and crying. Do NOT mention Victoria and earring songs.
8. Refuse to yield Kathleen's name even under torture.
9. Accept any consequence without complaint. Even if I am grounded for a month!

I wrote this action plan as soon as I got home on Friday.

But I didn't need it. No one noticed my scarf or tried to find out what it was covering up.

Eva and Isabel gulped their dinners and hurried off to a lacrosse game and a school play rehearsal.

Alex was invited to a movie with his friends.

Mom had to run off to a meeting.

Dad was cooking, loading the dishwasher, and figuring out how to juggle all the pick-ups and drop-offs of the next two days.

On Saturday no one in my family commented on my headband. On Sunday no one said a word about the hat I was wearing.

How come????

Aren't they just a teensy bit suspicious?

Don't they wonder why I'm hiding my ears?

WHERE is their curiosity?

Or do they think the scarves, hats, and headbands are part of my new sixth-grade look?

They have to discover my pierced ears sometime, don't they?

Don't they? DON'T THEY?

Or can I keep my earlobes hidden from my family forever?

That would be a universe-shattering, record-breaking event for the Hayes Book of World Records!

I feel <u>so</u> grown-up with my ears pierced. I practically feel older than Eva and Isabel!

In school, I will uncover my ears. HOORAY! I can't wait to see the look on Victoria's face!

When she sings that song, I'll hold my head high and march past with my new earrings on display.

I'm not an ear-piercing fake anymore!

Standing in front of the school bathroom mirror, Abby stripped off her headband and pulled her hair back into a ponytail. She twisted an elastic band around it several times, then stood back to survey the results.

You couldn't miss the gold post earrings. They sparkled and gleamed and practically shouted from her earlobes.

With a sigh of satisfaction, Abby reached into a zippered backpack pocket, found a tube of tinted lip gloss, and applied it generously to her mouth.

The bathroom door swung open. The girl with the

long wavy dark hair entered and approached the mirror. Today she was wearing a brilliant coral-colored blouse with a pair of velvet patched jeans and leather boots.

The girl glanced at Abby, smiled shyly, then looked away. Suddenly, she understood. This girl was even more scared of sixth grade than she was. And she was shy, too.

Abby slipped the tube of lip gloss back into its hiding place. She swung the pack onto her shoulders and glanced at her reflection in the mirror one final time.

In the mirror, the girl looked back. She looked as if she wanted to say something.

"Bye," Abby said.

The girl ducked her head. "Bye," she whispered.

The first bell rang, and Abby slid into her seat in homeroom.

"Glittering gold, Hayes!" Casey cried from the seat behind her.

"You like my earrings?" Abby said.

"They blind the eyes with their brilliance."

"I wonder what Victoria will say," Abby said.

"She'll be speechless," Casey predicted. "She won't be able to stammer out a simple 'like, you know.' "

In math class, Abby kept touching the gold earrings and drifting off into daydreams. In social studies, she could barely pay attention.

"Where *were* you?" Hannah asked at the end of class. "You seemed a million miles away."

"I was thinking about Victoria," Abby answered. "And what she's going to say when she sees me today."

"Are you worried?"

"Yes and no." Abby took a breath. "I'm armed with my golden earrings."

"*Armed* with *earrings?*" Hannah repeated.

"Sort of, I guess. You know!"

Both girls began to laugh. The friendly sound of Hannah's laughter followed Abby down the hall after they had parted again.

Abby's heart pounded as she approached her English classroom. This was the class she had with Victoria. Her steps slowed. She clutched her notebook more tightly.

She saw a flash of bright coral as the girl with the long dark hair slipped into the room. More students hurried inside, but Abby continued to wait at the door.

"Where *are* they?" Abby whispered.

Victoria and her friends were nowhere in sight. Were they waiting for her inside?

She took a deep breath and entered the classroom.

Chapter 12

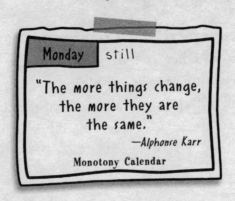

When I entered the English classroom, Victoria was in her seat. She was rubbing her eyes and sniffling a little.

I stared at her. Was Victoria <u>crying</u>? No, it was probably allergies.

Brianna sat a few seats away from her. She hummed as she checked her lipstick in a small gold mirror.

Then Victoria saw me. Her eyes glittered. "Abby Hayes and the clip-on craze," she chanted nastily.

"My earrings are real," I began, but Brianna interrupted.

74

"Don't you have anything better to do than pick on people?" she hissed at Victoria.

I stared at her in amazement. Was Brianna sticking up for me?

"Shut up!" Victoria said to her. "Who asked <u>you</u>?"

"Many people consult my opinion," Brianna said. "I'm considered wise beyond my years."

"Like, big deal."

"My sleepover party was fabulous," Brianna announced. "It was the best. We watched movies in my home theater. We had gourmet popcorn and individual boxes of specially wrapped chocolates for every girl."

"Who cares?" Victoria said.

"Next weekend we're all going to Tonya's house. It's going to be the <u>best</u> party. Except for mine, of course. Are you invited?"

"Who'd, like, want to go?"

"Everyone who's anyone," Brianna said smugly. "Only the best of the best."

Victoria's eyes flashed. "That's what <u>you</u> say."

Ms. Schmidt was writing this week's homework assignments on the board. "Okay, enough talking, everyone! Class is about to begin."

Brianna sat up in her seat and smiled eagerly at the teacher.

With an angry scowl, Victoria slammed a notebook on her desk. She caught my eye and snapped, "What are _you_ staring at?"

I didn't say anything. I took out my personal narrative essay.

"Abby Hayes, the one-earring wonder," Victoria sneered.

"I'm wearing two earrings, Victoria," I announced. "Real earrings, not clip-ons. I got my ears pierced this weekend."

"_SO?_" Victoria said.

There was nothing to say to that, so I said nothing.

(If I didn't feel so miserable, I'd give Victoria an award in the Hayes Book of World Records for Supremely Sarcastic Use of Single Syllable and Most Dramatically Disdainful _So_. But she's so mean that I'll

give her an empty page with a big red X
drawn across it instead.)

After she had finished writing this week's
assignments on the board, Ms. Schmidt collected our personal narrative essays. I had
written mine about watching Wynter and
how I learned to speak up when something
is wrong.

My sisters and parents keep telling me
how well I handled that difficult time with
Wynter.

So how come I can't handle Victoria?
It doesn't seem to make any difference
what I say or do. She just keeps on picking on me.

Yes, I have pierced ears. But nothing else
has changed.

Chapter 13

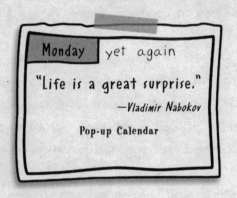

Monday yet again

"Life is a great surprise."
—Vladimir Nabokov

Pop-up Calendar

I wish it were.

Abby's "Great Surprise" Wish List
Here are the surprises I wish would happen:

1. Victoria would stop teasing me.

2. My parents would give me permission to have my ears pierced <u>right</u> <u>away</u> (so I wouldn't have to hide my earrings anymore).

3. Everyone in sixth, seventh, and eighth grade would forget everything that Victoria has ever said about me.

4. They would also forget about my fall.
5. The shy girl from English class would talk to me. We'd have a real conversation.

I've already thought of these surprises. So, would they really be surprises if they happened?

Or is a REALLY great surprise waiting for me? Something that I can't even imagine? I hope so!!!

"Guess what?" Alex asked at dinner on Monday night.

Eva passed Isabel a bowl of broccoli. "It's healthy for you," she insisted.

Her twin took an extra baked potato instead.

"Tell us your news," Paul Hayes said to his son.

Alex sat up and ran his fingers through his hair, leaving a streak of tomato sauce. "We're recreating an early American village in our classroom. We're going to dress up in costumes and pretend that we lived two hundred years ago! I got voted mayor!"

"Congratulations," Olivia Hayes said. "That's very impressive, Alex."

Isabel waved pale peach nails in the air. "I have some exciting news, too. I'm trying out for the lead role in the school musical, and I joined the debate team again. My honors classes are the best."

"So?" Eva cried. She handed a platter of roast chicken to her mother. "I've just been voted captain of the lacrosse team. I'm the first sophomore ever to be elected. I'm going to run for Student Council, and I'm chairing a drive for the athletic scholarship committee."

Abby stared at her plate. She had stopped eating when her brother and twin sisters had begun to recite their accomplishments. After all their honors and awards, what did *she* have to say for herself?

You won't believe it, everyone. I can find my way around Susan B. Anthony without getting lost.

I turned in all my homework today.

I never forget my locker combination.

I didn't cry when Victoria teased me.

No, she'd *never* admit to her superior siblings that Victoria was teasing her.

"Abby?" her father said. "How's middle school treating you?"

"Um, yeah . . ." Abby said. "It's okay, I guess."

Compared to her siblings, she sounded like the most dull and boring person in the world. She'd have to give herself a page in the *Hayes Book of World Records* for Utterly Uninteresting Utterances.

"Tell us," her mother urged. "I'm sure you've done something marvelous today, too."

"I, um . . ." Abby stammered.

Actually got a bathroom pass from the social studies teacher who doesn't like to give them out?

"I forgot to mention, I'm vice president of the Honor Society this year," Isabel announced.

"Well . . ." Abby began again.

"My teacher said that I should enter my robots in a national science fair," Alex added. "She thinks they're good enough to win a top prize."

"I . . ."

"And I'm going to make the all-state athletic roster," Eva said.

Abby dropped her fork with a clatter. Enough was enough. "I have exciting news, too," she said loudly.

"Have you won a writing award in your first week of school?" her father asked.

"No," Abby said, "nothing like that."

Her siblings and parents gazed at her with curiosity.

"*This* is my news." Abby tore off her hat. She yanked back her hair and pointed to her ears.

"Look!" she cried. "I got my ears pierced!"

Chapter 14

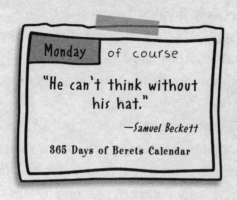

Monday | of course

"He can't think without his hat."

—Samuel Beckett

365 Days of Berets Calendar

Uh-oh. My hat is off. My secret is out.

Eva gasped and Isabel shrieked as Abby unveiled her earlobes.

Paul Hayes frowned, and Alex said, "Huh?"

"You did *what*?" Olivia Hayes said. Her lips pressed together in a thin line. "You got your ears pierced? Without permission?"

Abby nodded. Her heart was pounding, and her face felt hot.

"*Why*, Abby?" her mother asked. "Why would you deliberately break a family rule?"

"Because," Abby said, and then stopped. She couldn't say another word.

Olivia shook her head. " 'Because' is not an explanation."

"I . . ." Abby began. "I . . ." All of her carefully prepared arguments seemed to have vanished. She certainly wasn't going to tell them the truth. She'd *never* admit that Victoria had been taunting her for days.

"I can't believe you got your ears pierced on your own, Abby," Isabel said. There was a faint note of admiration in her voice. "When did you do it?"

"A few days ago."

"You've kept a secret for that long?" Eva said in astonishment.

"I keep lots of things secret," Abby retorted.

Her sisters gazed at her with new respect. But her parents looked angry.

"I'm very upset that you did this behind our backs," Olivia said. "I don't think you should have pierced ears at age eleven."

"Who needs two holes in the head?" Alex joked. But no one laughed.

"*Everyone* has pierced ears in sixth grade," Abby said defensively.

"I raised you to think for yourself," her mother said. "I'm disappointed in you, Abby."

"But I *did* think for myself!" Abby protested. "And now you're mad about it!"

Paul frowned. "Who did it?" he asked.

Abby didn't answer.

"I hope it wasn't one of your friends," Olivia said. "If your ears get infected, you can pay the doctor bill out of your savings."

"I'm taking good care of them!" Abby said. "They *won't* get infected."

Paul leaned back in his chair and looked at his wife. "The teen years are here." He sighed.

"Abby, your father and I will have to discuss this in private."

"I'll take any consequence," Abby said defiantly.

Olivia got up from the table. "We'll speak to you later. Don't think you're going to get away scot-free."

"She's not a criminal," Isabel protested. "She just pierced her ears."

"Against the family rules, with full knowledge," Paul said.

Paul and Olivia went upstairs to talk privately.

"Boy, oh, boy. You're in big trouble, Abby," Alex warned as he left to play with his robots.

"*So?*" Abby said. "It was worth it."

"You have guts," Eva said, almost grudgingly.

"Now that Mom and Dad are gone, tell us where you got it done," Isabel cried. "I'm dying to know!"

Abby took a deep breath. "I am not allowed to reveal my sources."

"Okay, never mind," Isabel said.

"You're taking good care of them, right?" Eva suddenly demanded.

"Yes," Abby said. "I've heard it a million times. You don't need to boss me around."

"Sorry," Eva and Isabel both said.

Abby couldn't believe it. Her older sisters were both apologizing to her?

"This is why you've been wearing hats at dinner every night," Isabel said.

"Of course," Abby said. "Earring cover-up."

"We thought it was sixth-grade weirdness," Eva said.

"Middle school makes people do strange things," Isabel added.

"Like what?" Abby asked carefully. She wondered if Victoria was a case of "sixth-grade weirdness."

"I wanted to skip sixth grade," Isabel confessed. "And go straight to seventh."

"You *did*?" Abby said. "Why?"

"I hated the first three months of sixth grade," Isabel said.

"You did?" Abby cried in astonishment. "How come you never told me?"

"Mom told me not to scare you." Isabel looked at her twin. "Remember when I walked out of school?"

"Don't get any bright ideas, Abby," Eva warned.

Abby shrugged. She wasn't going to walk out of school anytime soon. "What made you hate sixth grade so much, Isabel?"

"Because . . . it was . . . sort of . . . well . . ." Isabel, who was never at a loss for words, was at a loss for words.

"She didn't like the cliques," Eva explained, "and they didn't like her, either."

"They seemed so phony to me," Isabel explained. "And everyone wanted to be just like them. It was like the entire sixth grade had turned into mindless worshippers of the Popular People."

"The Popular People," Abby repeated slowly. "Have you ever heard of a book called *Sixth Grade Revealed*?"

Isabel looked startled. "How did you hear about *that*?"

"I found it in one of your throwaway boxes."

"Isabel was really mad when she wrote it!" Eva said.

"*You* wrote it?" Abby said. "Isabel?"

Isabel nodded. "They were teasing me every day in the halls. It was only for a few weeks, but it seemed like a lifetime."

"Yeah," Abby said, "I know what you mean."

"Writing the book made me feel a lot better."

"Tell Abby what you did," Eva ordered her twin.

"My plan was to publish and distribute *Sixth Grade Revealed* throughout the school." Isabel stared at her fingernails for a moment. "But then something funny happened."

"*What?*" Abby asked. Maybe Isabel would give her a clue as to how to deal with Victoria.

"I became friends with one of the popular kids," Isabel admitted. "And then the rest began to accept me. I discovered that many of the Popular People were actually nice."

Abby let out a long breath. This wasn't what she was hoping to hear. "Did you ever pick on kids who weren't popular?"

"*Never!*" Isabel said. She got up from the table. "You can turn around any situation," she concluded.

"Great," Abby mumbled. Isabel had obviously never met up with someone as vicious as Victoria.

One thing was for sure. Abby wasn't going to befriend Victoria anytime soon. And she couldn't see herself becoming a Popular Person, either.

But things had changed for Isabel. Maybe they'd change for her, too.

Chapter 15

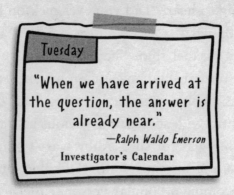

Tuesday

"When we have arrived at the question, the answer is already near."
—Ralph Waldo Emerson
Investigator's Calendar

Question: How can I make Victoria stop tormenting me?

Answer:

I have arrived at the most important question in my life right now. **Where is the answer?**

"**A**bby! You're not wearing a hat!" Hannah cried as Abby emerged from her house on Tuesday morning.

She clapped her hand over her mouth. *"Sorry!"* she whispered. "I hope no one heard me!"

Abby pushed back her red hair to show off the gold posts in her ears. "Don't worry," she reassured her friend. "It's not a secret anymore."

"They found out?" Hannah gasped.

"I told them."

"And . . . ?"

"My parents got really mad." Abby shrugged. "But it was worth it."

Hannah nodded approvingly. "Are they grounding you?"

Abby shook her head. Her parents had handed down their verdict before she had gone to bed last night.

"I have to do community service," she said. "My mother is organizing a winter clothing drive. I've promised to sort donations with her every Saturday afternoon for the next six weeks."

"Not too bad."

"It's better than scrubbing bathroom floors or not being able to go to a friend's house after school," Abby said.

"Maybe I'll help out, too," Hannah offered.

"Great!" Abby cried. "That would be fun!"

"Did they find out who did it?"

"They asked, but I didn't tell," Abby said proudly. "I *promised* Kathleen. She trusted me."

As they approached the school, Abby scanned the sidewalk and lawns. The area appeared to be Victoria-free. Abby breathed a sigh of relief.

There was just Brianna, holding court in the center of a group of adoring girls.

"The director *loved* me," Brianna boasted to her audience. "He said I was the *best*. Next time I'll have an even bigger and better role."

"Ooooooh," her fans crooned.

"How do you get better if you're already the best?" Abby murmured to Hannah.

"Best, bestest, most best?" Hannah suggested. The two girls walked into the school.

"I don't think Ms. Schmidt would agree."

"You're so lucky you have her for English," Hannah said. "Mr. O'Brien makes us memorize long lists of vocabulary words every night. And he mumbles in class. We haven't had *any* writing assignments yet."

"That sounds awful," Abby sympathized. She glanced at her reflection in the glass door of the library. Her gold earrings gleamed.

"He's a nightmare straight out of *Sixth Grade Revealed*."

"Hannah!" Abby cried. "I almost forgot to tell you!" She grabbed her best friend's arm and lowered her voice. "Isabel *did* write it."

"*Isabel? Sixth Grade Revealed?*"

"She hated sixth grade."

"Seriously?"

"She even skipped school once."

Hannah's eyes widened. "I don't believe it."

"It's true," Abby said. "And I would never have found out if I hadn't told everyone about my pierced ears. It was *so* worth it, Hannah. Even though my parents were really angry."

"They're not still mad, are they?" Hannah said. "Even after you agreed to the community service?"

"My mom is still a bit upset," Abby admitted. "But my dad made a joke. He said, 'No tattoos, Abby, okay?' "

"*Ugh,*" Hannah said. "Tattoos."

"He doesn't have to worry!" Abby cried. "I'd never get one of *those*!"

The first bell rang. The two friends separated and headed to their homerooms.

The girl with the long dark hair was hurrying

in the opposite direction. When she saw Abby, she glanced away.

Abby realized she had never seen her with another person. Did she have a single friend in the school? Having no friends would be worse than having one enemy. Abby suddenly felt grateful for all her good friends.

As Abby approached her homeroom, she saw Victoria at the end of the corridor. A small group of whispering girls surrounded her. She stepped forward when she saw Abby.

"Show everyone your *nice* pierced ears," Victoria commanded in a nasty voice.

Her friends snickered.

"They're so, like, totally adorable," Victoria taunted.

Abby glanced at Victoria and the girls who surrounded her. Suddenly, Abby was angry. She straightened, turned, and walked away.

"Hey! Come back here!" Victoria ordered.

As Abby hurried toward her homeroom, she heard Victoria crying out to her friends.

"Like, what's the matter with *her*? Can't she, like, take a joke?"

Abby didn't look back.

Chapter 16

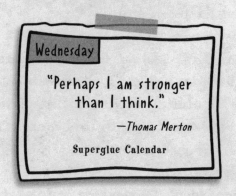

Wednesday

"Perhaps I am stronger
than I think."

—Thomas Merton

Superglue Calendar

When I hurried away from Victoria, I
felt scared. Was she going to run after me
or say something even meaner? But she
didn't do anything. She didn't even understand why I walked away.

Is that pathetic, or what?

I felt really good when I walked into
my homeroom. Casey smiled at me. "You look
happy today," he said.

"I just walked away from Victoria," I announced. "I don't care what she says anymore, I'm not sticking around to listen to it."

"Wow," Casey said. "That's great!" He gave me two thumbs-up.

Victoria was waiting for me outside Ms. Schmidt's class again. I walked right past her as if I didn't even see her. Then I went up to Ms. Schmidt and asked her if I could change my seat.

"What's the problem?" she asked.

"Someone keeps teasing me," I said.

Ms. Schmidt nodded. "Go find another seat."

I looked around the room. Mason was joking with a couple of boys in the back. Brianna was squirting perfume on her wrist. There were a lot of kids I didn't know. Suddenly, I saw the girl with the long dark hair. There was an empty seat across from her. I sat down in it.

She was doodling on a piece of paper.

I tore a piece of paper from my notebook and made a funny sketch of the school. I drew a smiley face on the bottom. Then I folded it up and tossed it on her desk.

She opened the note and looked at it.
Then she wrote something on the paper and
tossed it back to me.

She had drawn a flower on the bottom.

I smiled at her. "My name is Abby," I
said.

She smiled back like she really meant it.
"Sophia," she said.

The AMAZING DAYS of ABBY HAYES

Abby Hayes has some NEWS.

I can't believe it. I've graduated from 5th grade! YEAH! Even though I'll miss a lot of things from 5th grade (especially Ms. Bunder), I am SO ready to begin middle school.

Top 3 most EXCITING NEWS in my life:
1.) New school and teachers
2.) New friends
3.) **MY NEW WEBSITE**

I don't want to ruin ANY surprises, especially abou my new website. CHECK IT OUT! I promise that you'll think it is as cool as I do.

www.scholastic.com/abbyhayes

Love,

Abby   (p.s. see ya online ☺)

SCHOLASTIC

HAVE AN ABBY DAY

Meet Abby Hayes, your typical amazing fifth grader and the star of a series that's as fresh and funny as Abby herself!

Make your own calendar on Abby's Web site....
www.scholastic.com/titles/abbyhayes

Have you read them all?

■ SCHOLASTIC

ABBO

Three Girls in the City

Three unlikely friends
ONE BIG CITY

❑ 0-439-49839-2	Three Girls in the City: Self-Portrait	$4.99 U
❑ 0-439-49840-6	Three Girls in the City: Exposed	$4.99 U
❑ 0-439-49841-4	Three Girls in the City: Black and White	$4.99 U
❑ 0-439-49842-2	Three Girls in the City: Close-Up	$4.99 U

Available Wherever You Buy Books or Use This Order Form

Scholastic Inc., P.O. Box 7502, Jefferson City, MO 65102

Please send me the books I have checked above. I am enclosing $_____ (please add $2.0■ to cover shipping and handling). Send check or money order–no cash or C.O.D.s please.

Name_____Birth date_____

Address_____

City_____State/Zip_____

Please allow four to six weeks for delivery. Offer good in U.S.A. only. Sorry, mail orders are not available to residents of Canada. Prices subject to change.

■ SCHOLASTIC